·LAURA·RANKIN·
Fluffy and Baron

SCHOLASTIC INC.
New York Toronto London Auckland
Sydney Mexico City New Delhi Hong Kong

ISBN: 978-0-545-23833-5

12 11 10 9 8 7 6 5 4 3 2 1   10 11 12 13 14 15/0

Printed in the U.S.A.   40

First Scholastic printing, January 2010

Designed by Nancy R. Leo-Kelly
Text set in Bitstream Carmina
The art was prepared with acrylics and ink on Arches watercolor paper.

For Mom and Dad, with love

One summer day, someone new waddled into Baron's life. Her name was Fluffy.

Baron had to share his food with her . . .

and his water.

Every day, the two of them played together.
Baron was good at tag.
Fluffy was great at hide-and-seek.

Both of them were terrific at squirrel-chasing
and fly-snapping.

As the summer passed, Fluffy grew bigger and bigger.

By autumn, she was a full-grown duck.

She and Baron stayed close and warm together all winter long.

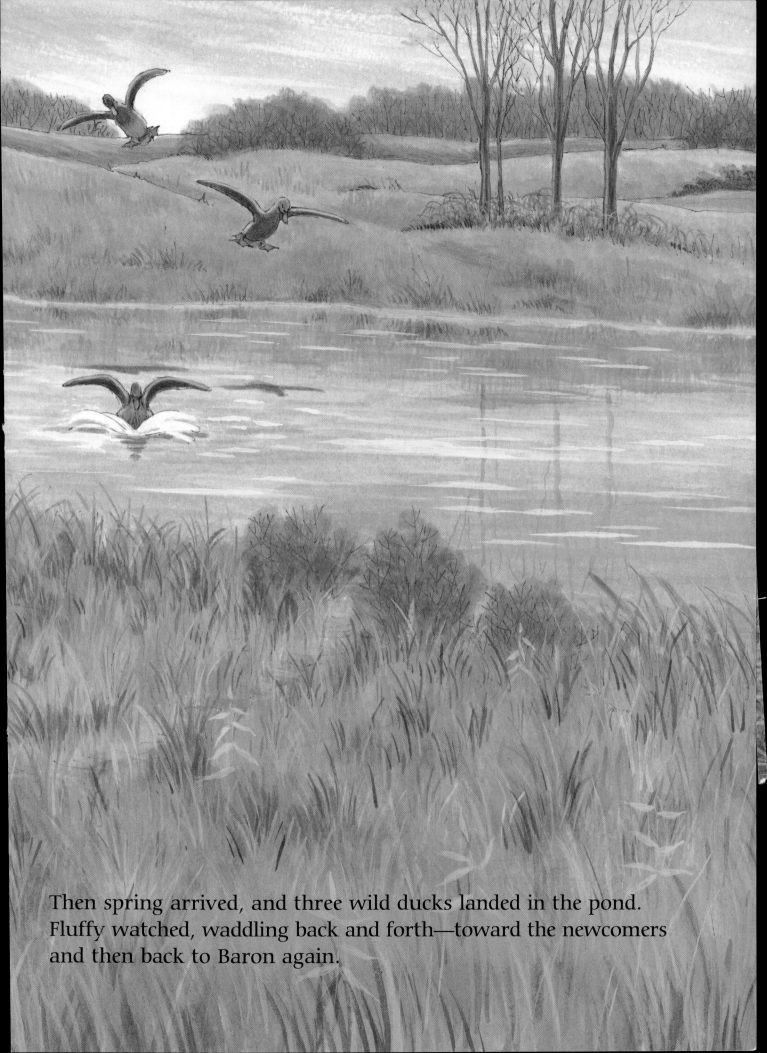

Then spring arrived, and three wild ducks landed in the pond. Fluffy watched, waddling back and forth—toward the newcomers and then back to Baron again.

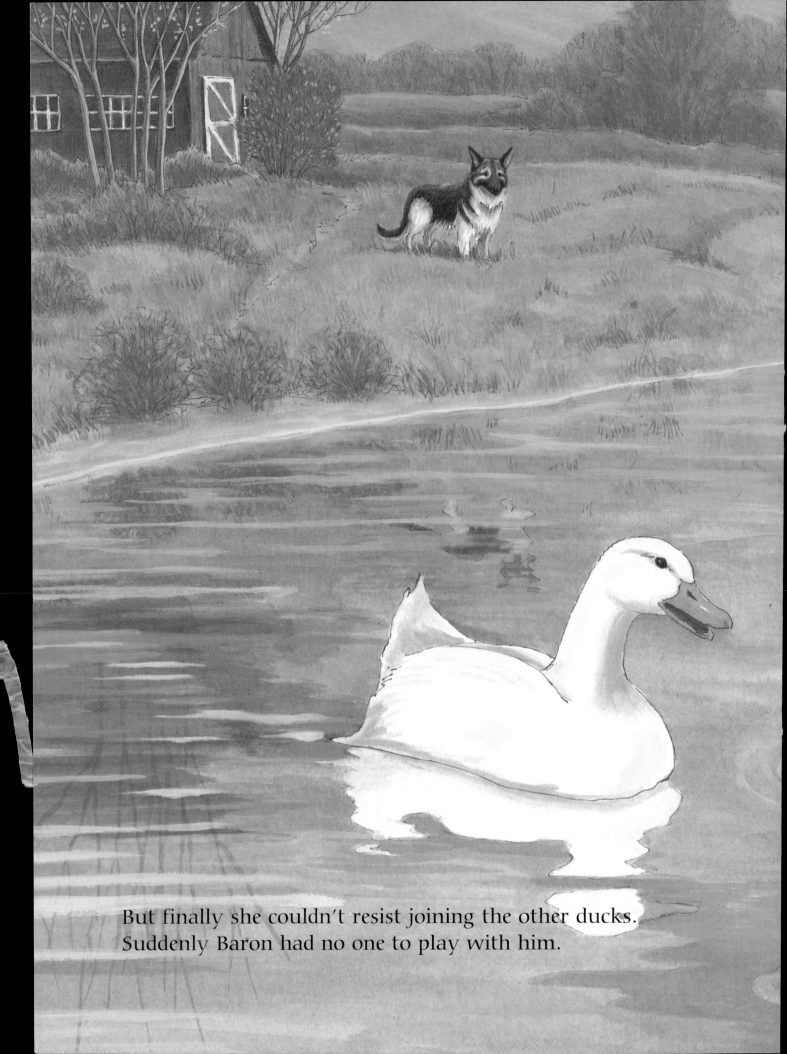

But finally she couldn't resist joining the other ducks.
Suddenly Baron had no one to play with him.

When it was time for dinner, Fluffy still hadn't returned. Baron had to eat alone.

For the next three nights, Fluffy didn't curl up with Baron in their favorite sleeping place.

Then the wild ducks flew away.

Baron tried to play with Fluffy, but she was too busy making a nest. She laid nine eggs in it, then gently settled herself on top and waited for them to hatch.

Four weeks later, there were ducklings!

Fluffy wanted Baron to
be the first one to meet them.
Baron's tail wagged and wagged.
Fluffy's wagged a lot too.

At last it was time to play again. And oh, what fun they all had!

That evening Baron led the way to dinner.

Never had he shared a happier meal.

And after such a busy day, everyone was eager to snuggle in together and fall asleep. Baron felt cozy and warm in his

favorite sleeping place, with nine brand-new friends and
best of all, his old friend Fluffy.

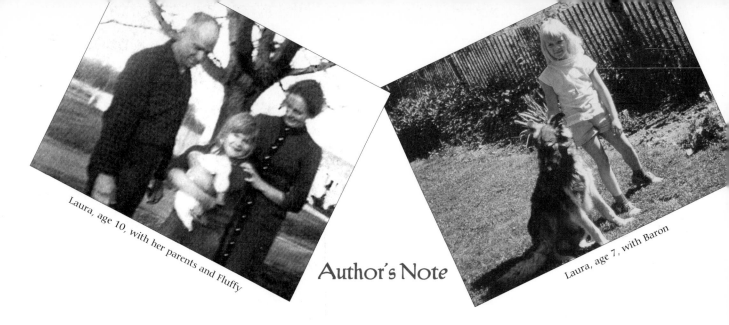

Laura, age 10, with her parents and Fluffy

Author's Note

Laura, age 7, with Baron

Fluffy and Baron *is based on many happy memories of my childhood pets, who really were best friends. Baron was a long-haired German shepherd and Fluffy was a Pekin duck.*

Pekins are a breed of domestic duck related to the Mallard. In the story, Mallard ducks are the wild ducks who visit the pond. Mallards can be found throughout the world, and although wild, are very adaptable. Some even raise their young in human habitats like city ponds, lakes, and reservoirs.

Mallards mate in the spring. A Mallard hen (female) can lay eggs for about eleven to seventeen days after mating with a male. She finds a sheltered spot near a pond, lake, or other wetland area, and makes a nest of grasses lined with her soft, downy feathers. Then the hen lays one egg each day until there are between seven and twelve eggs. She sits on—incubates—the eggs, leaving the nest only briefly for food and water, until the ducklings hatch twenty-eight to thirty days later. The drake (male duck) only stays with the hen through about the first week of incubation; male Mallards do not help to raise their young.

Soon after the ducklings hatch, usually between late April and late May, their mother teaches them how to swim, forage for food, and hide from predators. Ducklings grow rapidly; within two months their newborn down has been replaced by adult feathers and they are ready to fly.

Mallards are migratory birds. In late September and October the fall migration begins. The ducks fly from their northern breeding grounds to spend the winter in warmer wetland and coastal areas where food supplies are more plentiful. Many birds fly almost without a break. Others (such as Fluffy's visitors in this story) stop to rest and eat during the long journey. Then in February and March, the spring migration begins and the Mallards head north, once again returning to their breeding grounds.

There are many differences between wild ducks and domestic ducks like Fluffy. Mallard ducks and other wild species have lean bodies, strong, long feathers, and powerful muscles built for flight. They are born with all the natural instincts needed for survival in nature. Domestic ducks are bred to have heavy bodies and are often not capable of flight. Domestic ducks, like all pets, have been bred to rely on humans for their care, food, and shelter. It is extremely difficult for them to survive in the wild.